MY BIG GIRL POTTY

by JOANNA COLE
illustrated by MAXIE CHAMBLISS

HarperCollinsPublishers

Watercolors were used for the full-color illustrations.
The text type is 18-point Cooper Light.

My Big Girl Potty
Text copyright © 2000 by Joanna Cole
Illustrations copyright © 2000 by Maxie Chambliss
Manufactured in China.

For information address HarperCollins Children's
Books, a division of HarperCollins Publishers,
195 Broadway, New York, NY 10007.

www.harperchildrens.com

Library of Congress Cataloging-in-Publication Data
Cole, Joanna.
My big girl potty / by Joanna Cole; illustrated by Maxie Chambliss.
p. cm.
Summary: Ashley learns to pee and poop in her potty and makes the transition from diapers to big-girl pants.
Includes tips for successful potty teaching.
ISBN 0-688-17041-2
[1. Toilet training—Fiction.]   I. Chambliss, Maxie, ill.   II. Title.   PZ7.C67346 My 2000
[E]—dc21   99-50287

15 16 SCP 20 19

❖

Ashley is a girl just your age.

Ashley likes playing with toys
and looking at books.
Do you like those things, too?

Ashley wears diapers.
Do you wear diapers, too?

When Ashley's diaper is wet or dirty,
she tells her mommy or daddy.
Then they put a new diaper on,
and Ashley is clean and dry again.

One day, Mommy and Daddy
brought home a big box.
Do you know what was inside?
It was a new potty for Ashley.

Ashley tried sitting on the potty
with her clothes on.
Ashley's bunny Floppy sat
on the potty, too.
It was fun!

Mommy took off Ashley's diaper.
She said, "Let's have potty time.
When you need to make pee-pee
or poop, please sit on the potty."

After a while, Ashley's daddy said,
"Try sitting on the potty.
Maybe some pee-pee will come out."
Ashley sat and sat.
But nothing went into the potty.

Later, Ashley read her books.
"Try sitting on the potty," said Mommy.
"Maybe some poop will come out."
Ashley sat and sat.
But nothing went into the potty.

Ashley played with her toys.
Daddy said, "Try the potty again."
Ashley sat and sat.
This time something happened!

Mommy and Daddy and Ashley
looked in the potty. They saw pee and poop.
"Ashley used her potty!" said Mommy.
She hugged and kissed her.

Mommy helped Ashley wipe herself.
Daddy helped her pour the
pee and poop into the big toilet.
Ashley flushed the toilet.
The pee and poop went into
pipes under the house.
Then Ashley washed her hands.
"What a big girl you are!" said Daddy.

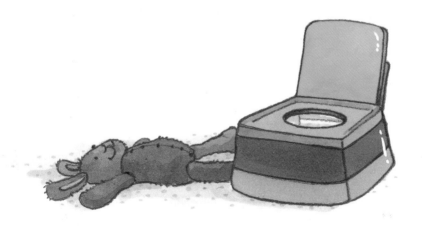

At bedtime, Mommy put a diaper on Ashley.
"You'll still need a diaper at night for a while,"
said Mommy.

In the morning, it was potty time again.
Mommy took off the diaper,
and Ashley used her potty.

Every day Ashley had potty time.
One day Mommy said, "Now you are
very good at using your potty.
It's time for big-girl pants."
Mommy and Ashley went to the store.
They picked out special big-girl underpants.

At home, Ashley put the pants on.
When she used the potty, she pulled
the pants down. Ashley liked to keep
her new pants clean and dry.

One day Ashley forgot to use her potty.
Her pants got wet. The floor got wet, too.

"Don't worry," said Daddy. "All children
have accidents sometimes."
Mommy helped Ashley clean up.
She gave her clean pants.
"Next time you'll remember," she said.
And do you know what?
Next time Ashley did!

You can be like Ashley.
You can learn to use the potty, too.

Then won't you be proud of yourself!

Tips for Successful Potty Teaching

- Don't rush! Most children are not completely trained until around twenty-eight months. Some are earlier, some later.

- Get ready by telling your child that urine and feces come from her body. Help her learn to make the connection between the feelings of elimination and what comes out of her body.

- Wait for one or more of the following signs of physical and emotional maturity: Your child's diaper stays dry for a few hours at a time; she tells you when she is about to urinate or have a bowel movement; she asks to use the potty.

- Start by having a few hours of "potty time" every day or so. Remove the diaper and request that your child use the potty.

- Give friendly reminders to encourage success.

- Praise your child for *trying,* as well as for succeeding. Never scold or punish.

- Expect accidents! They are the best way for your child to learn that without a diaper she must use the potty.

- When your child is using the potty consistently, switch to underpants.

- Use a diaper at nap time and bedtime until your child is dry.

- Make your expectations clear: You are confident that your child will learn.